NOODLE the DOODLE

Steals the Show

Jonathan Meres

With illustrations by
Katy Halford

To Becca.
Welcome to the clan.

First published in 2021 in Great Britain by
Barrington Stoke Ltd
18 Walker Street, Edinburgh, EH3 7LP

www.barringtonstoke.co.uk

Text © 2021 Jonathan Meres
Illustrations © 2021 Katy Halford

The moral right of Jonathan Meres and Katy Halford to be
identified as the author and illustrator of this work has been
asserted in accordance with the Copyright, Designs and
Patents Act, 1988

A CIP catalogue record for this book is available
from the British Library upon request

ISBN: 978-1-80090-018-9

Printed by Hussar Books, Poland

CONTENTS

CHAPTER 1
Welcome to Wigley

The day began like every other day at Wigley Primary. But it wasn't like every other day. Because Mr Reed had some big news.

"Good morning, everybody!" Mr Reed boomed. He was standing at the front of the class. A dog was standing next to him. His name was Noodle. Noodle the doodle.

"Goooooooood mooooooooooorning, Mis-ter Reeeeeeeeeed!" sang all the children.

"WOOF! WOOF! WOOF! WOOF!" said Noodle.

"Gooooooooood mooooooooooorning, Noooooooooooooooooodle!" sang the children.

"WOOF!" said Noodle. "WOOF! WOOF! WOOF! WOOF! WOOF!"

"That's right, Noodle," said Mr Reed. "I *do* have some important news. Thank you for reminding me."

"WOOF!" said Noodle. He looked very pleased with himself. He was wagging his tail and panting. His tongue was hanging out. It looked like a slice of wet pink ham.

Marty put his hand up.

"Yes, Marty?" said Mr Reed.

"Can you really understand what Noodle says?" said Marty.

"Don't be stupid," said Josh. "He's just pretending!"

"That's mean, Josh," said Nora.

"Sorry, Marty," said Josh.

"That's OK," said Marty.

"Excuse me, Mr Reed?" said Shakira. "Please can you tell us what the important news is?"

Mr Reed smiled.

"Of course I can, Shakira," he said.

Everybody sat up and listened. The last time Mr Reed had important news was when he told the pupils that they were going to the seaside. And that had been one of the best days ever. They had played crazy golf. And Noodle had run off with a sausage. So what was *this* news going to be? Everyone wanted to know.

"Is it your birthday, Mr Reed?" said Sol.

Mr Reed smiled. "No, Sol," he said. "It isn't my birthday."

"You always ask that, Sol," said Callum.

"So?" said Sol. "One day I'll be right!"

Mr Reed spotted Lou's hand in the air. "Yes, Lou?" he said.

"Are we going to start reading a new book, Mr Reed?" said Lou. Her eyes were shining. Reading was her favourite thing in the world. Especially if she was curled up reading on a beanbag with Noodle.

"No, Lou," said Mr Reed. "Not today. But I'm glad you think reading is important."

"Ooh, ooh, Mr Reed, Mr Reed!" said Abdul. His hand was in the air. He was jumping up and down in his seat.

Callum laughed. "I think someone needs the toilet," he said.

"I don't need the toilet!" said Abdul. "But I think I know what Mr Reed's important news might be."

Everyone turned and looked at Abdul. He seemed excited. Did Abdul know? the pupils wondered. Or was he just guessing?

"Well, Abdul?" said Mr Reed.

"Is there a new member of class?" said Abdul.

"Correct!" said Mr Reed. "Well done, Abdul!"

"Oooooooooooh!" said all the others. That really *was* important news! There hadn't been a new member of class since Noodle the doodle had arrived! And that was ages ago.

Mr Reed looked at the big clock on the wall. "He should be here any moment," he said.

"Ooooooooooh!" said everyone. So the new classmate was a boy. What would he be like? they wondered. Would he be funny, like Sol? Would he love playing football, like Josh? Or would he be into science and inventing stuff, like Nora?

There was a knock at the door.

"WOOF!" said Noodle the doodle. He was excited too.

Mr Reed walked to the door and opened it.

A boy was standing outside. A woman was standing next to him, holding a baby.

"Welcome to Wigley Primary," said Mr Reed. "Please come in."

The woman and the boy entered the classroom. But the boy didn't look at anyone. He was staring at the floor. He seemed shy.

"Boys and girls," said Mr Reed. "I'd like you all to say good morning to Samir."

"Goooooooood mooooooooooorning, Samir!" sang the children.

"And this is Samir's mum," said Mr Reed.

"Goooooooood mooooooooooorning, Samir's mum!" sang the children.

Samir's mum smiled. "Hello," she said.

"And this is Samir's baby sister," said Mr Reed.

"Goooooooood mooooooooooorning, Samir's baby sister!" sang the children.

Samir's baby sister giggled. But Samir was still staring at the floor.

"WOOF!" said Noodle. "WOOF! WOOF! WOOF!"

Samir looked up. He saw Noodle. Noodle began wagging his tail like crazy. It smacked a wastepaper bin and made a sound like a drum.

"I think Noodle likes you, Samir," said Lou.

Samir didn't say anything. But he smiled. He thought everyone at Wigley Primary seemed very nice.

CHAPTER 2
Pizza Pals

Samir's mum and baby sister stayed for a while. But then it was time for them to go. Samir looked a bit sad. His mum hugged him and said something. She spoke in a soft voice. No one else could hear what his mum said. But Samir didn't look so sad now.

Samir's mum opened the door to leave. She smiled and waved. Samir waved back. Then his baby sister did a burp. Everyone laughed. The door closed and Samir's mum was gone.

"Excuse me, Mr Reed?" said Marty.

"Yes, Marty?" said Mr Reed.

"There's a space next to me," said Marty. "Samir could sit there."

"Ooh, yes!" said Shakira. "Can he, Mr Reed? Please?"

Shakira sat at the same table as Marty.

"Please, please, pleeeeeeease?" said Abdul.

Abdul sat next to Shakira.

"Hmm," said Mr Reed. "That's a very good idea, Marty."

"WOOF!" said Noodle the doodle. "WOOF! WOOF! WOOF!"

"What's that, Noodle?" said Mr Reed. "You think it's a good idea too?"

"WOOF!" said Noodle one more time.

Mr Reed looked at Samir. "What do *you* think, Samir?" he said. "Would *you* like to sit with Marty and Shakira and Abdul?"

Samir didn't reply. He looked as if he was thinking. Then Noodle trotted over. He sat on the floor next to Marty. Noodle looked at Samir. He started to wag his tail again. It thumped on the floor.

"WOOF! WOOF!" said Noodle the doodle.

Samir smiled. He walked to the table. He sat down next to Marty. He gave Noodle a stroke. Noodle lay down and rolled onto his back.

Marty grinned. "Noodle wants you to tickle his tummy," he said to Samir.

Samir tickled Noodle's tummy. Noodle stretched out his legs. He was very long. It

looked like Noodle was flying. It made Samir
laugh.

"Do you like macaroni cheese, Samir?" asked
Shakira.

Samir nodded.

"Shakira is bonkers about macaroni cheese," said Marty. "It's all she ever thinks about!"

Shakira laughed.

"No, it's not!" she said. "I just like it, that's all."

"What's your favourite food, Samir?" said Marty.

Samir looked at Marty for a moment.

"Pizza," he said. This was the first time he'd spoken.

"Pizza?" said Marty. "Me too!"

"Yeah!" said Shakira. "Pizza pals!"

Samir laughed. "Pizza pals," he said.

Shakira and Samir did a fist bump.

"Do you like numbers, Samir?" said Abdul.

Samir looked at Abdul.

"I love numbers," said Abdul. "Adding up. Taking away. Multiplying. Dividing. Numbers are cool!"

"OK, then," said Marty. "What's twelve pizzas divided by four, Abdul?"

Abdul grinned. "Three pizzas," he said. "Easy-peasy!"

"Easy-pizza," said Samir.

Shakira laughed. "Good one, pizza pal!" she said.

Shakira and Samir did another fist bump.

"Mmmm, yum," said Marty. "Three pizzas!"

Mr Reed smiled. He had been watching. He was pleased to see that Samir was getting on with the others. Mr Reed wanted him to

feel welcome. Moving to a new school could
be scary.

"OK, guys," said Mr Reed. "Who would like to
do some drawing?"

Lots of hands shot up in the air.

"Excellent!" said Mr Reed. "Noodle?"

"WOOF!" said Noodle. He stood up and began
wagging his tail.

"Here, boy!" said Mr Reed, and patted his leg.
Noodle the doodle trotted over to him.

"Sit," said Mr Reed.

Noodle sat.

"Good boy," said Mr Reed. He took a stack
of paper from his desk. He put it in Noodle's
mouth. "Now give all the boys and girls a sheet
of paper."

Noodle trotted from table to table. He stopped at each one. All the children took a sheet of paper. The paper was a bit soggy, but no one cared. Noodle loved to help.

"OK," said Mr Reed. "Now I'd like you all to draw something that makes you happy."

Everyone started to draw. Mr Reed walked around the classroom. He stopped behind each pupil.

Nora drew a picture of a rocket zooming into space.

"That's nice, Nora," said Mr Reed.

Lou drew a picture of her grandma's house.

"That's lovely, Lou," said Mr Reed.

Sol drew a picture of a bike.

"That's splendid, Sol," said Mr Reed.

Mr Reed stopped behind Samir's table. "How are we getting on over here?" he asked.

"Good thanks, Mr Reed," said Marty. "I'm drawing a pizza. Because pizza makes me happy."

Mr Reed looked at Marty's drawing. "That's marvellous, Marty," he said. "I can almost smell it!"

Then Mr Reed looked at Samir's drawing. Samir was drawing a dog. It had shaggy golden curly fur, a black button nose and a bushy tail. Its tongue was hanging out. It looked like a slice of wet pink ham.

"Wow!" said Mr Reed. "That's *very* good, Samir!"

Everyone crowded round to look at Samir's picture.

"It's amazing!" said Josh.

"It's fantastic!" said Callum.

"It's Noodle," said Samir.

"WOOF!" said Noodle from under the table. He was having a rest. Carrying the paper to everyone had made him tired.

"Noodle makes you happy?" said Lou.

Samir nodded.

"Me too," said Marty.

"Me three!" said Sol.

Samir laughed. He looked down. Noodle was licking his hand. Samir laughed because it tickled.

CHAPTER 3
A Brilliant Idea

Soon it was time for morning break.

Josh, Lou, Callum and Abdul all played football. Josh and Lou were one team. Callum and Abdul were the other. Josh and Lou's team won. The score was 37–29.

Nora and Sol played on the climbing frame. They hung upside down from the bars and pretended to be bats.

Shakira did some hula-hooping. She made the hoop whizz around her tummy so fast it was just a blur.

Marty and Samir threw a tennis ball to each other. But Noodle kept jumping up and catching it in his mouth. They called the game "doggy in the middle". Noodle barked and wagged his tail. He thought that it was the best game ever. He didn't want it to stop.

But then the bell rang. Break was over. Everyone went back inside.

"OK, everyone," said Mr Reed. "Listen carefully now. I have something else to tell you."

Everyone sat up in their chairs. Noodle sat up on the floor. Mr Reed had something else to tell them? What would it be? But there was no time for anyone to guess. Because Mr Reed told them.

"You know that every year our school raises money for charity," said Mr Reed.

"Oooooh!" said everyone. Well, *nearly* everyone. Samir didn't say it, because this was his first day at Wigley Primary. He didn't know about these things yet. But all the other children were very excited. They loved to raise as much money as they could. And every year, they did it in a different way.

"So," said Mr Reed. "We have a big question. How are we going to raise money this time? Any ideas?"

Everyone started to think. Everything went silent. The only sound was the clock ticking.

Then Shakira put her hand up.

"Yes, Shakira?" said Mr Reed.

"We could bake cakes!" said Shakira.

"Yum!" said Callum.

"Not for us to eat!" said Shakira. "To sell!"

Callum grinned. "I'd get my mum to buy them all," he said. "And then I'd eat them!"

"Could I have one?" said Sol.

"What do you say?" said Callum.

"Please?" said Sol.

Callum grinned. "Just one," he said.

"Any other ideas?" said Mr Reed.

"What about a read-a-thon?" said Lou.

"A *what*-a-thon?" said Josh.

"A *read*-a-thon," said Lou. "It's like a sponsored walk. But instead of walking, we read books instead."

"Hey, I know!" said Marty. "We could read books *and* walk at the same time!"

"Someone could walk into a lamp post!" said Nora.

"Good point, Nora," said Mr Reed. "That could be dangerous. But a read-a-thon is a fantastic idea, Lou."

Everything went silent again. You could almost hear everyone thinking.

"I know!" said Abdul at last.

"Yes, Abdul?" said Mr Reed.

Abdul smiled. "We could have a talent show," he said.

"Ooh!" said Callum. "You mean like the ones on TV?"

"Yes!" said Abdul.

"Hey, I know what we could call it," said Shakira. "Wigley's Got Talent!"

"That's brilliant!" said Mr Reed.

"WOOF!" said Noodle. "WOOF! WOOF! WOOF! WOOF! WOOF!"

"What's that, Noodle?" said Josh. "You think it's brilliant too?"

Everyone laughed. Even Samir.

CHAPTER 4
Important Things

There was great excitement at Wigley Primary that day. The pupils were buzzing like bees. There was going to be a talent show! People would pay to come and watch it. Then all the money would go to charity.

There was just one problem. Wigley Primary was a very small school. There were only two classrooms. And the assembly hall was tiny. Not many people would be able to come if they did the show there. Then they wouldn't raise very much money. There was only one solution. They would have to find somewhere bigger. And there was only one place bigger in Wigley – the village hall. Lots of people would be able to watch if they did the show there. And then lots of money would be raised.

The village hall was like a real theatre. There was a stage. And curtains. And spotlights. It was perfect. It was going to be so much fun.

"We must make posters!" said Nora.

"Good idea!" said Sol.

"Yes," said Shakira. "We could stick a poster up outside the school!"

"And one in the shop," said Josh.

"And one in the library," said Lou. The library was Lou's favourite place.

"Yeah!" said Sol. "Then loads of people will come!"

"Excellent!" said Mr Reed. "But what else do we need to think about to plan the show?"

Everybody had a think. Well, nearly everybody. Noodle was so excited that he'd fallen asleep. He was dreaming about sausages.

"Well, guys?" said Mr Reed. "What else?"

"Refreshments," said Shakira.

"Pardon?" said Callum.

"Food and drink!" said Shakira.

Callum looked confused. "For us?" he said.

"No!" laughed Shakira. "Not for us! For the audience!"

"Oh, right," said Callum.

"What else?" said Mr Reed.

They all did some more thinking.

"Ooh, I know!" said Abdul. "We'll need someone to sell tickets!"

"Yes, very good, Abdul," said Mr Reed. "We will. And what else?"

"We'll need to *make* the tickets," said Nora.

"That's right, Nora," said Mr Reed. "We will. But we're forgetting something. Something *very* important."

"What is it, Mr Reed?" said Sol. "Please may we have a clue?"

Mr Reed smiled. "What's the show going to be called?" he asked.

Josh was first to put his hand up.

"Yes, Josh?" said Mr Reed.

"Wigley's Got Talent!" said Josh.

"Correct!" said Mr Reed. "Wigley's Got *Talent!*"

"Oh, I know!" said Lou. "We need to think about what we are all going to do in the show."

"Well done, Lou!" said Mr Reed. "What are your skills? What are you good at? What are your *talents*?"

It was a good question. No one had thought about that yet. They'd been too busy thinking about other things. But without performers there would be no show.

"Excuse me, Mr Reed?" said Marty. His voice was quiet. He looked worried.

"Yes, Marty?" said Mr Reed. "What is it?"

"Do we *have* to do something?" said Marty. "In the show, I mean."

Mr Reed looked at Marty for a moment. He knew that some children were confident and *liked* performing in front of other people. But not all children did. Some were shy. And that was OK. Everyone was different.

"No, Marty," said Mr Reed. "You don't *have* to do anything. No one *has* to."

Mr Reed smiled. Marty looked relieved.

"Hey, Marty!" said Shakira. "Your job can be to open and close the curtains!"

"Yeah," said Callum. "And switch the lights on and off!"

"Yeah," said Abdul. "Those things are really important."

Mr Reed looked at Marty.

"Well, Marty?" he said. "What do you think? Would you like that?"

Marty nodded. "Yes," he said. "I'd like that very much. Thank you."

"Fantastic," said Mr Reed. "And how about you, Samir?"

Samir had been quiet too. He was stroking Noodle. Noodle was lying underneath his desk. He was still asleep.

"Would *you* like to do something in the show, Samir?" said Mr Reed. "Do *you* have any special talents?"

Samir thought for a moment. Noodle stretched and yawned and made a funny squeaking sound.

"Maybe," said Samir.

CHAPTER 5
Crash!

Days went by. Then a week went by. Then another week went by. And another. And another. And another.

Life carried on as normal at Wigley Primary. Books were read. Stories were written. Drawings were drawn. Sums were worked out. But all the while, everyone was thinking about something else. They were thinking about Wigley's Got Talent.

A date had been picked. The village hall had been booked. Posters had been put up. Tickets were selling fast. And something even more important had happened. Nearly everyone knew what they were going to do in the show.

Josh loved to play football. So he was going to do some tricks. He would keep the ball up in the air. He would kick it and head it. It was called doing "keepy-uppies". Josh's record was forty-three. He was going to try to do fifty!

Sol was funny. He liked to make people laugh. His grandma said that he should be a comedian. So he was going to tell some jokes.

Lou had a small voice when she spoke. But it was very different when she sang. When Lou sang, she had a big voice. And she loved to sing. So that was what she was going to do.

Abdul was going to do a magic act. His dad was a bus driver. But he also knew how to do

magic tricks. He taught some of them to Abdul.
Abdul thought his dad really was magic.

Shakira's favourite thing was macaroni
cheese. Her second favourite thing was dancing.
So that was what she was going to do. But she
wasn't going to do it alone. Callum and Nora
were going to dance with her. They would do
street dance. The music would be very loud.
People would think they were from a big city,
not a tiny village. It would be so cool.

The only pupil who didn't know what to do
was Samir. Samir wasn't keen on dancing. And
he didn't like singing very much. He didn't
know many jokes. He could only do a few
keepy-uppies. So what *could* he do? What was
his talent? Time was ticking on. Samir had to
decide soon. The day of the show was getting
nearer.

Samir liked coming to school. He hadn't
been sure at first. But now he didn't mind when
his mum dropped him off. He was friends with

everyone. He joined in with their games. The other pupils made Samir feel welcome. But his *best* friend was Noodle the doodle. Noodle made Samir happy.

One morning, everyone was hard at work. Samir was sitting next to Abdul. They were multiplying and dividing numbers. The class was very quiet. There were only two sounds. The sound of the clock ticking and the sound of Noodle snoring.

Then there was a loud crash from the hall. Noodle woke up. He hid under Samir's chair. He was scared. He was shaking. He made a whimpering noise. But the crash had only been the sound of a pot being dropped on the floor. Shakira's mum was the school cook. She was getting the hall ready for lunch. But Noodle didn't know that. He thought that something bad had happened.

"It's OK, boy," said Samir. He spoke in a soft voice. Noodle stopped whimpering. He rolled

39

onto his back. Samir tickled Noodle's tummy. Noodle wagged his tail.

Then Samir had an idea. He reached into his backpack. He pulled out a small plastic container. Samir opened it. It was full of blueberries. He took one out and offered it to Noodle. Noodle ate it. His tail began wagging like crazy.

"WOOF!" said Noodle. "WOOF! WOOF! WOOF!"

"What's that, Noodle?" said Samir. "You'd like another one?"

"WOOF!" said Noodle.

Samir smiled. He gave Noodle another blueberry. And then another. And then another.

"Samir?" said Mr Reed.

Samir looked up. He hadn't noticed Mr
Reed standing next to him. He'd been too busy
thinking. And he'd just had another idea.

"Are you OK?" asked Mr Reed.

Samir nodded. At last he'd decided what
to do. He knew what his talent was. All he
had to do now was practise.

CHAPTER 6

Come Back with That Microphone!

It was the day before the show. Everyone had been practising very hard. So far, they'd been practising at home. Now it was time to practise all together. They were going to have a rehearsal and perform their acts. But they were going to do it without an audience.

It was important that Marty knew what to do. He needed to practise opening the curtains. He needed to practise switching the lights on and off. It didn't matter if anything went wrong during the rehearsal. Because there was no audience there to see it.

The children walked from the school to the village hall. Noodle was on a lead that Samir was holding. It wasn't very far. But Noodle kept stopping to pee on every single lamp post.

"I wish I could do that," grinned Sol.

"What?" said Josh. "Pee on a lamp post?"

"Aw, yuk!" said Nora. "That's disgusting!"

"It's a natural thing to do," said Callum.

"Yes," said Shakira. "If you're a dog!"

They all laughed.

At last they arrived at the village hall. There was a big poster on the door. It was a poster for the show. Everyone was very excited when they saw it.

"Let's go, guys!" said Mr Reed. He opened the door and went into the village hall. Noodle ran after Mr Reed, pulling on his lead. Samir got pulled along behind him.

"Whoa!" yelled Samir. "Slow down, boy!"

But Noodle didn't slow down. It was his first time in the village hall. He was excited too. Samir let him off his lead and he started whizzing around. There were lots of new things for Noodle to sniff. And he sniffed every one of them.

"WOOF!" said Noodle. "WOOF! WOOF! WOOF! WOOF! WOOF!"

Mr Reed clapped his hands. "OK, everyone!" he said. His voice was loud. It boomed around the hall. "Let's get cracking!"

Noodle stopped whizzing around. He sat down. He was panting. His tongue was hanging out. It looked like a slice of wet pink ham.

There were some steps at the side of the stage. Marty climbed up them. He vanished behind the curtains. He pulled on a rope and the curtains opened. Then Marty switched the lights on. There was a microphone in the middle of the stage in a stand. The microphone sparkled in the light.

"Oooooooooooooooh!" said all the other pupils. They were even more excited now.

Josh was the first to practise his act. He ran onto the stage holding a football. He bounced it. He kicked it into the air. Then he did some keepy-uppies. But the most he did was four. Josh looked a bit sad.

"It's OK, Josh," said Lou. "You'll be great tomorrow."

Then Sol practised some jokes. But he couldn't remember them.

"Don't worry, Sol," said Shakira. "You'll remember them tomorrow."

Then Lou practised her song. She was singing along to some music. Marty pressed a button to play the music. But it was the wrong song.

"Sorry, Lou," said Marty.

Lou tried to smile. "It's not your fault, Marty," she said.

Abdul was the next to practise. All his tricks kept going wrong. He tried to pull a toy rabbit out of his hat. But he pulled out a banana instead.

"Oh, no!" said Abdul. "What if that happens tomorrow?"

"Don't worry, Abdul," said Sol. "I'll eat it."

Shakira, Callum and Nora were next to practise. The music blasted out. They started to dance. But everything went wrong. They kept bashing into each other. The other pupils thought it was part of their act. But it wasn't.

Samir was the last to practise. Only Mr Reed knew what Samir was about to do. He hadn't told anybody else. He was still a bit shy. Samir walked onto the stage. Everybody looked at him. But he didn't say anything.

"Are you OK, Samir?" said Mr Reed.

Samir nodded and said something. But his voice was very quiet. No one could hear him.

Mr Reed smiled. "Would you like to use the microphone?" he said. "It will make your voice louder."

Samir nodded again. He took the microphone out of its stand.

"Here, boy," said Samir into the microphone. Mr Reed was right. This time everyone could hear him.

Noodle the doodle dashed onto the stage. He saw Samir holding the microphone. But Noodle

thought it was a sausage. Noodle jumped.
He flew into the air like a furry rocket. He
snatched the microphone from Samir's hand.
Then he jumped off the stage and headed for
the door.

"NOODLE!" yelled Marty. "COME BACK WITH
THAT MICROPHONE!"

But Noodle didn't come back. He was having
way too much fun. If the children wanted the
microphone, they'd have to catch him first!

Noodle the doodle ran outside. Everyone
chased after him. They had to get the
microphone back. Noodle might break it.
Or he might dig a hole and bury it. If that
happened, the show might not go ahead.

There was a park next to the village hall.
Noodle started whizzing around it with the
microphone in his mouth. First he whizzed one
way. Then he whizzed another way. His tail

was wagging like crazy. He thought it was the best game ever.

Everyone ran after Noodle. Well, not *everyone*. Samir was standing still. He took something out of his pocket. It was a small plastic container. He opened it. He took out a blueberry and held out his hand.

"WOOF!" said Noodle. He was still whizzing about. "WOOF! WOOF! WOOF!"

"Here, boy," said Samir.

Samir's voice was quiet. But Noodle stopped whizzing. He looked at Samir. Then Noodle ran towards him.

"Sit," said Samir.

Noodle sat.

"Drop it," said Samir.

Noodle dropped the microphone onto the grass.

"Good boy," said Samir.

Samir put his hand under Noodle's mouth. Noodle ate the blueberry. Samir picked up the microphone.

The others were watching. They were amazed.

"Wow!" said Shakira.

"Awesome!" said Sol.

"Brilliant!" said Nora.

"Magic!" said Abdul.

"Well done, Samir!" said Mr Reed.

Samir smiled. The show would go on after all!

CHAPTER 7
Wigley's Got Talent!

At last it was the day of the show. The pupils had arrived at the village hall. They were waiting in a small room at the side of the stage. Everyone was excited. But they were also nervous. Did Wigley have talent? It was time to find out.

Mr Reed clapped his hands. "Everyone," he said. "May I have your attention, please?"

They all looked at Mr Reed. He had their attention.

"Thank you," Mr Reed said. "Whatever happens tonight, there's something I want you to know. And no, Sol. It's *not* my birthday!"

Everyone laughed. Even Sol.

"Good one," said Sol.

"What is it, Mr Reed?" said Nora.

Mr Reed looked at Nora and smiled. "I'm very proud of you all," he said. "You've all worked very hard. So, well done!"

"WOOF!" said Noodle the doodle. "WOOF! WOOF! WOOF!"

"What's that, Noodle?" said Mr Reed. "You think everyone should go out there and enjoy themselves?"

"WOOF!" said Noodle, wagging his tail. "WOOF! WOOF! WOOF!"

Everyone laughed again. By now the audience had arrived in the hall. They were sitting in their seats. It was time for the show to begin.

Mr Reed walked out onto the stage. He spoke into the microphone.

"Good evening, ladies and gentlemen!" Mr Reed's voice boomed around the hall. "Welcome to Wigley's Got Talent!"

The audience clapped and cheered.

"We have a fantastic show for you tonight!" said Mr Reed. "And remember, all the money that we raise will go to charity!"

The audience clapped and cheered again.

"And now," said Mr Reed. "Please give a big warm Wigley welcome to our first act of the evening … Josh!"

Marty was sitting at the side of the stage. He pressed a button. The curtains opened. Marty pressed another button. Some music began to play.

Josh jogged onto the stage. He was dressed in his football kit and was holding a football. He bounced it a few times. Then he started doing keepy-uppies. He kicked the ball with his left foot and his right foot. He didn't do fifty keepy-uppies. He did twenty-six before the ball fell to the ground. But no one cared.

"Ooooooh!" said the audience. But Josh hadn't finished yet.

Marty pressed a button. The music stopped and everything went quiet. Josh bounced the ball a few more times. Then he did a big kick. The ball rose high into the air and nearly touched the ceiling. When it came back down, Josh caught it on the back of his neck. Then he flicked the ball into the air and caught it. Then

he bowed. Everyone clapped and cheered. Josh waved and jogged off the stage.

Josh joined the other pupils standing at the side of the stage. They'd all been watching him.

"Wow, Josh!" said Callum. "That was fantastic!"

Josh smiled. "Thanks," he said.

Sol was the next to perform. He walked onto the stage and pretended to trip up. Everyone laughed. Sol smiled and spoke into the microphone.

"Knock, knock," he said.

"Who's there?" said the audience.

"Boo," said Sol.

"Boo who?" said the audience.

"There's no need to cry," said Sol.

Everyone laughed again.

"What's brown and sticky?" said Sol.

"We don't know!" said a voice in the audience.

"A stick!" said Sol.

Everyone laughed again.

Sol told three more jokes. Then he bowed. The audience clapped and cheered. Sol walked off the stage and pretended to trip again. Everyone laughed even louder than the first time.

"See?" said Shakira. "I told you it would be OK."

Sol smiled. "Thanks," he said.

Then it was Lou's turn to perform. She walked onto the stage and took the microphone from the stand. But Lou wasn't looking at the audience. She was looking at her feet. Then Marty pressed a button. Some music began to play. Lou looked up. Then she started to sing. Her voice was loud and clear. It filled the hall.

The other pupils watched from the side of the stage. They turned and looked at each other. They were amazed. Lou seemed like a completely different person when she was singing.

The song finished. Everyone clapped and cheered. Lou bowed and walked off the stage.

"That was brilliant, Lou!" said Josh.

Lou smiled. "Thanks, Josh," she said. Lou's voice was quiet again. But she seemed very happy.

The next act was Abdul. He came onto the stage wearing a top hat. He did some magic tricks. First he did a trick with some playing cards. Then he made a coin vanish. Then he took the hat off. He put his hand inside the hat and pulled something out. But it wasn't a

banana. It was a rabbit. Not a real rabbit – a
glove puppet. The puppet bonked Abdul on the
head with a magic wand. Everyone laughed.

Abdul and the puppet bowed. The audience
clapped and cheered as Abdul walked off the
stage.

"That was great, Abdul," said Josh.

"Hey, Abdul," grinned Sol. "Can you make my homework vanish too?"

Shakira, Callum and Nora were the next to perform. They walked out onto the stage wearing baseball caps. Shakira's was sticking out to one side. Nora's was sticking out to the other side. Callum was wearing his back to front. They folded their arms and stared at the audience. They were trying to act cool, so they didn't smile.

"One, two, three, four!" yelled Shakira.

Marty pressed a button. Some loud music started blasting out. Shakira, Callum and Nora began to dance. Sometimes they all did the same dance move. Sometimes they did different things. Shakira spun around on her back. Nora moved like a robot. Callum did a backflip!

"Whoa!" said Lou.

"Awesome!" said Sol.

Then Marty pressed a button. The music stopped. But Shakira, Callum and Nora didn't bow. They just stared at the audience and folded their arms again. But it didn't matter. Everyone still clapped and cheered.

And now there was just one more act to go.

CHAPTER 8
Noodle Steals the Show

Mr Reed walked onto the stage again. He took the microphone from its stand and spoke into it.

"Well, everybody," he said. "I think we can all agree. Wigley most definitely *has* got talent!"

The audience clapped. They cheered. They stamped their feet.

"What a show it's been!" said Mr Reed. "But it's not over yet. Because we still have one more act to go!"

"Ooooooooooooooh!" sang the audience. Everyone looked around as they tried to work out who it was.

"There are no judges here tonight," Mr Reed went on. "No prizes. No winners and losers. Tonight, *everyone's* a winner!"

The audience clapped again.

"But there's one person who deserves an extra-big Wigley welcome tonight," said Mr Reed. "Because this person has only been at the school for a very short time. So let's hear it for the one and only ... Samir!"

There was a great big cheer as Samir walked onto the stage. He stopped in the middle. He turned and looked at the audience. Everyone wondered what he was going to do. Was he going to sing? Was he going to dance? Was he going to tell jokes? The hall had gone silent.

Then a small voice shouted, "Samir! Samir! Samir!"

Samir looked down from the stage. He saw his little sister in the front row, sitting with his mum. She waved. Samir smiled. He waved back.

"Awwwwwwwwwww!" sang the audience.

Samir took something out of his pocket. It was a small plastic container. He opened it and took something out. It was a blueberry. Samir held out his hand.

"Here, boy!" said Samir.

Noodle the doodle trotted onto the stage. His tail was wagging. Everyone cheered.

"Sit," said Samir.

Noodle sat.

"Good boy," said Samir. He gave the blueberry to Noodle.

"High five," said Samir.

Noodle held up one of his front paws. Samir bent down and touched Noodle's paw with his hand. Everyone clapped. Samir gave Noodle another blueberry. But that was just the start of the act.

"Spin," said Samir.

Noodle spun around in a circle. First one way. Then the other way.

"Lie down," said Samir.

Noodle lay down.

"Roll over," said Samir.

Noodle rolled over. His paws were sticking up in the air. Samir tickled his tummy.

The other pupils were watching from the side of the stage. They were enjoying Samir's act just as much as the audience.

"Aw!" said Callum.

"So cute!" said Lou.

"So clever!" said Nora.

But Samir and Noodle hadn't finished yet. They still had one more trick to perform.

"Sit," said Samir.

Noodle sat.

Samir turned. He looked at Marty.

"Hoop, please," said Samir.

Marty rolled a large plastic hoop across the stage. Samir stopped it. He walked away from Noodle and held the hoop up.

"Drum roll, please," said Samir.

Marty pressed a button. There was the sound of a drum roll.

"Here, boy!" said Samir.

Noodle ran forward and jumped. He flew through the hoop like a furry rocket. The

audience clapped and cheered. Noodle turned around and ran back. He jumped through the hoop again.

"Sit," said Samir.

Noodle sat.

"Good boy," said Samir. He gave Noodle one last blueberry. Then Samir turned to the audience and bowed. Noodle was panting. His tongue was hanging out. It looked like a slice of wet pink ham. He looked very happy. And so did Samir.

The audience all clapped and cheered again. Samir and Noodle trotted off the stage. Noodle stopped next to the curtain. He sniffed it. Then he lifted his leg and did a pee. Everyone laughed. No one minded. Noodle had been such a good dog. And it was only a tiny bit of pee.

Mr Reed walked back out onto the stage. "Thank you all for coming tonight," he said.

"Let's hear it one more time for our wonderful acts!"

The audience clapped again as the children appeared one by one. They stood in a line across the stage.

"Josh!" said Mr Reed. "Sol! Lou! Abdul! Shakira, Lou and Callum! And of course – Samir and Noodle!"

"WOOF!" said Noodle. "WOOF! WOOF! WOOF! WOOF!"

"What's that, Noodle?" said Mr Reed. "We've forgotten someone very important?"

"WOOF! WOOF!" said Noodle. "WOOF! WOOF! WOOF!"

"Someone who's been working very hard tonight?" said Mr Reed.

"WOOF!" said Noodle. "WOOF! WOOF!"

"Of *course!*" said Mr Reed. "Thank you for reminding me, Noodle! Everyone please give a great big clap to Marty!"

Marty appeared from the side of the stage and joined the end of the line. The audience burst into more claps and cheers. Then all the pupils bowed. The show was over.

CHAPTER 9
A Nice Problem

"Good morning, everyone," said Mr Reed.

It was the day after the show. Everyone was very tired.

"Gooooooooooooood moooooooooooooooorning, Mis-ter Reeeeeeeeeeeeeeeed!" sang the children. They stretched out all the words even more than normal.

"Woof!" said Noodle. He tried to woof again. But the woof turned into a yawn. Then Noodle tried to wag his tail. But even his tail was tired.

All that whizzing about the night before had been exhausting.

Mr Reed smiled. "Well done, everyone," he said. "Last night was fantastic. You were all amazing! Did everyone have fun?"

"Yeeeeeeeeeeeees, Mis-ter Reeeeeeeeeeeeeeeed!" sang the children.

"Woof!" said Noodle. But the woof turned into another yawn. Noodle closed his eyes and fell asleep.

"I had no idea that you were all so talented!" said Mr Reed. "You should be very proud of yourselves."

The children looked pleased. They *were* proud of themselves. They'd worked very hard.

"And do you know what the best thing about the show is?" said Mr Reed.

Everyone thought for a moment. Then Sol put his hand up. He was grinning.

"Yes, Sol?" said Mr Reed.

"We don't have to do any work today?" Sol said.

Mr Reed laughed. "Very funny, Sol!" he said. "Anyone else?"

Shakira put her hand up.

"Yes, Shakira?" said Mr Reed.

"Does it mean that it's macaroni cheese for lunch?" she said.

"Yum, yum," said Mr Reed. "That *would* be nice, wouldn't it? But no, Shakira. That's not what I was thinking."

"Ooh!" said Lou. She put her hand up. "I know!"

"Yes, Lou?" said Mr Reed.

"All the money's going to charity?" Lou said.

"Exactly!" said Mr Reed. "Well done, Lou! All the money we raised last night is going to charity! And we raised a *lot* of money! Or I should say, *you guys* raised a lot of money!"

"Yeeeeeeeeeeeeeeeaaaaaaaaaaaaaaah!" sang all the children.

Mr Reed stopped smiling. He looked more serious. "There's just one problem," he said.

Everyone was surprised. What kind of problem could it be?

Mr Reed smiled again.

"Don't worry," he said. "It's a *nice* problem."

Callum looked confused. "A *nice* problem?" he said. "What do you mean, Mr Reed?"

Mr Reed looked around. He wondered if anyone had guessed what the nice problem was. Marty put his hand up.

"Yes, Marty?" said Mr Reed.

"Is the problem that we need to decide which charity to give the money to?" said Marty.

"Correct!" said Mr Reed. "Well done, Marty! Because there are all sorts of wonderful charities. So, which one should we give the money to?"

"Oh!" said Callum. "Now I see why it's a *nice* problem!"

"Exactly, Callum," said Mr Reed. "So, come on, then? Any ideas?"

Everyone did some more thinking. Nora was the first to put her hand up.

"Yes, Nora?" said Mr Reed.

"How about a charity that has something to do with climate change?" said Nora.

"Oooooh!" said Josh in a funny voice. He was making fun of Nora. "Something to do with climate change. Get you!"

Nora glared at Josh. "It's not funny!" she said. "Climate change is very important!"

"You're right, Nora," said Mr Reed. "Climate change *is* very important. Any other ideas?"

"My grandma's not very well," said Lou.

Sol looked at Lou. "What?" he said. "So you think we should give all the money to your grandma?"

"No!" said Lou. "I think we should give it to a charity which helps people with the same illness."

"Oh, right," said Sol. "Sorry about your grandma, by the way."

Mr Reed smiled. "That's a good idea, Lou," he said. "Anyone else?"

Abdul put his hand up. "We could give it to a charity that helps homeless people?" he said.

"Ooh, yes!" said Shakira. "That's a fantastic idea, Abdul."

"They're *all* wonderful ideas, Shakira," said Mr Reed. "But how about something a bit closer to home?"

The children looked puzzled. Closer to home? They wondered what that meant.

There was a sudden crashing noise in the kitchen. Noodle woke up and shot under Samir's chair. He was shaking. He thought something bad had happened. But it hadn't. Shakira's mum had just dropped another pot.

Samir reached down and stroked Noodle.

"It's OK, boy," said Samir in a quiet voice. Noodle soon stopped shaking. He rolled onto his back. Samir tickled his tummy.

"Samir," said Mr Reed. "Do *you* have an idea which charity we could give the money to?"

Samir thought for a moment.

"WOOF!" said Noodle the doodle. "WOOF! WOOF! WOOF! WOOF!"

"What's that, Noodle?" said Samir. "A charity which helps look after animals?"

"YEEEEEEEEEEEEEEEEAH!" sang all the other children. Now they knew what Mr Reed had meant by "closer to home". He meant an *animal* charity! It was a fantastic idea!

"WOOF!" said Noodle the doodle. His tail wagged like crazy. "WOOF! WOOF! WOOF! WOOF! WOOF!"

Because Noodle the doodle thought it was a fantastic idea too!